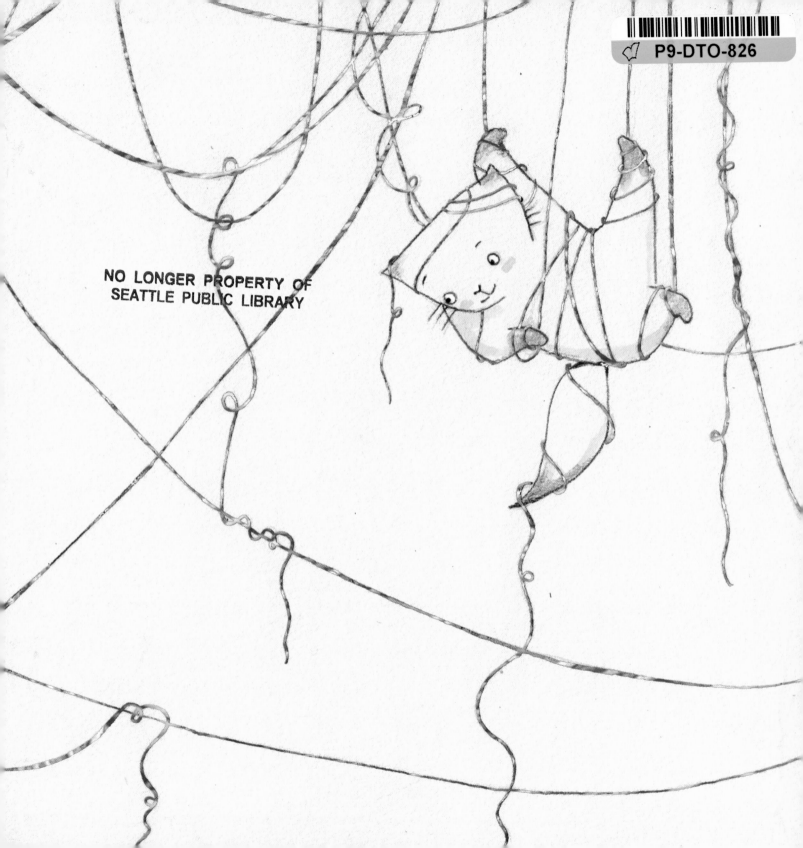

Mr. Fluffernutter

Jennifer Gray Olson

Alfred A. Knopf · New York

Mr. Fluffernutter and I
are best friends.

We love spending time together

doing all of our favorite things.

Today we are having a tea party!

Mr. Fluffernutter
LOVES tea parties!

Milk, sugar,
Mr. Fluffernutter?

After tea,
we play...
DRESS-UP!

Looking good,
Mr. Fluffernutter!

He enjoys getting fancy.

We have tons of fun
all morning.

Hey, where are you going,
Mr. Fluffernutter?

It seems like
Mr. Fluffernutter
would rather stare
at the fish today.

Okay, Mr. Fluffernutter.

You want WHAT for lunch,
Mr. Fluffernutter?!

And NOW you just want to play with your yarn?

Maybe Mr. Fluffernutter and I
AREN'T best friends after all.
Maybe we'll have more fun...

alone.

See, that's better.

Much better.

Yup.

Awwwww, Mr.

Fluffernutter!!!

Mr. Fluffernutter and I
BOTH really like bath time.

We just do it
a little differently.

Good night,
Mr. Fluffernutter.

For those who love us,
even at our most unlovable

THIS IS A BORZOI BOOK PUBLISHED BY ALFRED A. KNOPF

Copyright © 2017 by Jennifer Gray Olson

All rights reserved. Published in the United States by Alfred A. Knopf, an imprint of Random House Children's Books,
a division of Penguin Random House LLC, New York.

Knopf, Borzoi Books, and the colophon are registered trademarks of Penguin Random House LLC.

Visit us on the Web! randomhousekids.com

Educators and librarians, for a variety of teaching tools, visit us at RHTeachersLibrarians.com

Library of Congress Cataloging-in-Publication Data is available upon request.
ISBN 978-0-385-75496-5 (trade) — ISBN 978-0-385-75497-2 (lib. bdg.) — ISBN 978-0-385-75498-9 (ebook)

The illustrations in this book were created using pencil, watercolor, and digital collage.

MANUFACTURED IN CHINA
October 2017   10 9 8 7 6 5 4 3 2 1   First Edition
Random House Children's Books supports the First Amendment and celebrates the right to read.

Let me SLEEP, sheep!

Meg McKinlay

illustrated by
Leila Rudge

CANDLEWICK PRESS

Amos was counting himself to sleep.
He closed his eyes and smiled as fluffy
white sheep trotted away across the grass.

"One," he said. "Two."

Suddenly, there was a loud THUD.
And then another.

"Not again!" said the first sheep.
"I was in the middle of dinner."

"I was having my wool clipped,"
said the second. "Just look at me!"

"Counting us, are you?" said the first sheep.

Amos nodded. "Yes. And I was up to three,
so if you could just—"

"Just **what?**" said the first sheep. "Excuse me, but how would *you* feel if you were dragged into a strange bedroom and told to parade yourself around? We are *sheep*, you know. We have *names*. Mine is Felix, not, as you so rudely call me, 'One.'"

"These kids!" said the second sheep. "Why can't you count pigs every once in a while? Pigs have nothing better to do with their time." He sighed. "Oh, all right. Let's get on with it, then. Where's the fence?"

Amos frowned.
"The fence?"

Felix nodded. "If you want to count us, you need a fence. It's in the rules."

"Rules?" said Amos. "Wait . . . does it have to be a fence?" He looked around him. "Couldn't you just jump the cupboard or something?"

"The *cupboard*?" Felix shook his head. "Impossible! Walter here has a bad knee. And Judith is afraid of heights. They'd never make it."

"Judith?" said Amos. "Who's Judith?"

Felix stared back at him. "Judith is number seven. She'll be along shortly. If you ever get this fence organized, that is."

"Maybe we should just forget it." Amos yawned.
"I'm feeling sleepy now anyway."

"Oh no you don't!" said Felix.
"You've called us now. Until you
provide an officially approved fence,
this is where we live."

"And you may not realize," added Walter,
"that sheep can get very smelly.
Especially when we're wet."

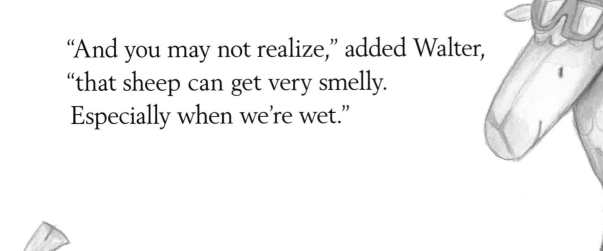

"I feel like having a shower right now,"
said Felix. "Which way is the bathroom?"

"Do you happen to have a hot tub?" asked Walter.
"I love those little bubbles."

"Ooh!" said Felix. "What an excellent idea.
I hope your parents won't mind."

Amos sighed. "All right.
I'll make you a fence."

And he set to work.

"Too low!" said Walter. "It's jumping, not hopping!"

"We are sheep," said Felix. "Not rabbits."

"Okay," said Amos. And he made it higher.

"Too high!" said Walter. "It's jumping, not leaping!"

"We are sheep," said Felix. "Not kangaroos."

"Okay," said Amos. And he made it lower.

"Too wobbly!" said Walter.

"One bump and that'll collapse," said Felix.

"Okay," said Amos. And he made it more stable.

"Too hard!" said Walter.

"We need a gentle landing," said Felix.

"Okay," said Amos. And he made it softer.

"Not to mention," said Walter,
"TOO THIRSTY!"

"Huh?" said Amos.

"I mean," said Walter, "that we'll be needing drinks. At the finish line."

"Finish line?" said Amos. "It's a fence, not a marathon!"

"Excuse me," said Walter. "Are *you* a sheep?
Do *you* know how hot it gets under this wool?"

"Especially," said Felix, "when we haven't been
properly clipped."

"Okay," said Amos.
And he got some water.

"Too **boring!**" said Walter.

"Needs more color," said Felix.

"Could you paint it?" said Walter.

"Maybe you could play some music," said Felix.

"Make it more like a dance party!" said Walter.
"I'm tired of jumping fences anyway."

"Now you guys are just being silly,"
said Amos. And he stepped back
to admire his fence.

"Not bad," said Felix. "You'll have to test it, of course."

"Me?" said Amos.

"We have to save our energy," said Walter, "for the big jump."

"Okay." Amos sighed.

And he jumped

and jumped

and jumped . . .

until he was so tired he could hardly . . .

"Oh," said Felix.

"Look at that," said Walter.

"Kids today!" said Felix.

"No stamina!" said Walter.

"Oh well," said Felix.
"Shall we call the others?"

"Let's," said Walter.
"They're going to *love* this."

"This," said Felix, "is the best fence ever."

For all the little lambs
M. M.

For Gene and Ina
L. R.

First U.S. edition 2019
First published by Walker Books Australia 2019

Library of Congress Catalog Card Number pending
ISBN 978-1-5362-0547-3

18 19 20 21 22 23 CCP 10 9 8 7 6 5 4 3 2 1

Printed in Shenzhen, Guangdong, China

This book was typeset in Berling.
The illustrations were done in mixed media.

Candlewick Press
99 Dover Street
Somerville, Massachusetts 02144

visit us at www.candlewick.com